FALLING FOR OXFORD

CONNOR WHITELEY

No part of this book may be reproduced in any form or by any electronic or mechanical means. Including information storage, and retrieval systems, without written permission from the author except for the use of brief quotations in a book review.

This book is NOT legal, professional, medical, financial or any type of official advice.

Any questions about the book, rights licensing, or to contact the author, please email connorwhiteley@connorwhiteley.net

Copyright © 2024 CONNOR WHITELEY

All rights reserved.

DEDICATION

Thank you to all my readers without you I couldn't do what I love.

CHAPTER 1
10th March 2023

Outskirts of Oxford, England

Finn Richards was so excited as he sat down the last of his large plastic boxes in the middle of the cold, dark brown wooden floor in his new living room. He had only bought the place a few weeks ago with his two best friends as they wanted to start living, working and enjoying Oxford. And Finn was just so glad he was finally moving in.

After so long of dreaming, wanting and lusting to be in Oxford, the city of dreaming spires, he was finally going to live here. Just like he had always wanted ever since he was a little kid.

Finn just grinned as he looked at the four large bare white walls around him. Sure the walls right now didn't look very attractive but there was so much amazing potential or maybe that was his undergrad degree in interior design talking, but walls were canvases to be honest.

Finn loved nothing more than crafted perfect rooms, perfect spaces and perfect places that really did reflect the people that lived in them.

Finn went over to the large floor-to-ceiling window that stretched along one side of the living room and smiled as his two best friends and all their parents finished unloading their cars. The three black SUVs on the drive probably made it look like a cottage belonging to mobsters but Finn didn't care.

Not only because there were so few people living on this main stretch of road that went straight into the heart of Oxford, but because this was his home and he loved it.

The air still had the nice new smell with hints of floor wax, vanish and a few other subtle chemicals because the estate agent had promised the house would be professionally cleaned before they moved in. Finn didn't mind at all considering the extreme estate agent fees he had to pay.

He liked hearing his friends and family laugh, chat and make jokes about all the guys and girls they were going to have over here. And Finn definitely couldn't deny that would be nice but he had known Joanna and Eli for over a decade and he knew the chance of any of them getting boys or girls back to the house was tiny.

But not impossible.

As Joanna came in, wearing her long black hoody and tracksuit bottoms (not that she knew how to exercise despite her slim figure), with two plastic boxes stacked on top of each other, Finn took the first one and almost died at the sheer weight of it all. Then he realised this was carrying her extreme library of books, and Finn was determined to find a great bookshelf or case for her.

In his experience it was always the little things that helped him to show how much his friends meant to him.

Eli just walked in with nothing and Finn laughed because it was so like Eli not to carry his own luggage and boxes. And a few moments later Eli's mum and dad stumbled in wearing matching black coats with a few boxes each.

"You spoil him too much," Finn said.

"Sadly we do," his dad said straining under the weight of the boxes.

Finn helped Eli's mum and dad with the boxes and as Joanna's parents and Finn's own parents joined them. He had to admit they had shitlots of plastic boxes in the middle of the living room and he wasn't sure the cottage was big enough for everything.

He really hoped it was.

"This is so exciting," Joanna shouted and Finn hugged his two best friends. They had lived together at university for the past three years and he couldn't wait to live with them for even longer.

They were brilliant people to live with, they didn't judge him for being gay and they had no problem with him bringing guys back to spend the night. Something he was really grateful for.

Finn's mother hugged him. "I'm so proud of you and if you need anything make sure you call me. And just call me once a week anyway,"

Finn kissed his mother on the cheek and hugged his dad tight. "I will. I love you both and thanks for helping us today,"

"We love you too," all the parents said to all of them as they headed back to their cars.

Finn had wanted them to stay the night and they could go out for dinner together in Oxford but there were a ton of accidents on the roads so it was going to take long enough to get home as it was. And the incoming storms weren't exactly going to help matters.

"Should we, you know, start unpacking?" Finn asked opening a box of their cooking stuff. He noticed a few pots and pans with some flowery designs on so they had to belong to Joanna.

Eli came over and hugged him and made Joanna join into the hug too. "This is going to be brilliant. Living again with my besties in a brand-new city,"

"This is going to be fun," Finn said, getting out some of the pots and pans so he could take stock of what they had and needed to buy in Oxford.

"And I have some news," Joanna said, "I got an email from that job agency and they're confirmed I've working that University of Oxford function tonight,"

Finn smiled at Joanna. That was brilliant news and it was good to know that that silly job agency that helped to get new people to the city part-time jobs was actually working.

He took out his phone and was surprised that he too had been accepted for the party tonight.

Finn stood up perfectly straight and just looked at the mountain of plastic boxes in front of him. Somewhere in that mountain was his black suit and tie for formal occasions and now he just needed to find it before tonight.

Not an easy job at all.

CHAPTER 2
10th March 2023
Oxford, England

Oxford University student Edward Lords sat under a massive conifer tree in the centre of Trinity College reading a fascinating new psychology paper on human perception. He had always enjoyed psychology, human behaviour and just learning in general and he loved Oxford even more.

From his little spot under the immense tree, he could admire the stunning ancient buildings of Trinity college with its stained glass windows, impressive masonry work and just enjoy the little slice of nature in the middle of Oxford.

Edward liked that it was still early March so there was a slight bite to the air that kept a lot of other students inside, and it meant they stayed away from him and he could just get some peace in amongst the chaos of everyday life going to one of the world's most elitist universities.

Edward watched as a cute guy wearing a full-on business suit walked through the college courtyard with his girlfriend as they laughed and kissed a little. That was probably the most physical contact he had seen between two people in public at Oxford for the past three years.

He had always known that Oxford was a great but very snobbish place, but it seemed that kissing in outside wasn't really allowed. A person could kiss indoors or in bedrooms but outside was a no-no.

Edward didn't understand it but as the cold wind gently howled past him, he realised it didn't really matter. In two months' time his exams would be done and he could be done of this great, wonderful place that had given him a ton of stuff.

Edward had loved how he had had so much contact with world-leading experts, gotten to take part in some brilliant research and the list of contacts he had gotten was well worth his tuition fees. Edward had loved every single second of his time here. Maybe except the odd homophobic comment but he didn't expect anything less from a place like Oxford.

And he was straight passing so it didn't matter. He just wanted to learn and enjoy his last two months here.

"Afternoon Ed,"

Edward smiled as Ivy and Claire came over to him and sat on the cold, slightly damp ground in long beautiful black dresses. They might have been sisters but Edward knew they were both amazing, funny and very different people in their own right.

He liked them even more because they were scholarship students like him, and their parents were poor as dirt and yet they thrived here.

Edward had to admit that Claire and Ivy probably thrived more than him, because Ivy was just scheming and she had managed to get Claire dating one of the snobbish rich men that got all three of them a lot of social protection, power and influence.

Something Edward rather liked.

"You ready for the party tonight?" Ivy said. "I already have a game plan sorted out,"

Edward smiled and just shook his head. He couldn't actually believe Trinity College was holding a fundraiser for the silly Liberal Arts programmes that were beyond pointless and that Ivy had seen this as an opportunity.

"He doesn't see the point," Claire said.

"I mean seriously? After knowing us for three great years you still don't understand how I scheme," Ivy said. "The plan my dear boy is simple, there will be plenty of rich, snobbish, posh boys at the party. They will drink, we will all become more attractive and they will be laid,"

"And I was thinking your scheming would be useful," Edward said.

Ivy grinned. "It is useful. Claire will be there with Albert and you and me need to get some dick too,"

Edward frowned and looked around to make sure no one was looking.

Ivy looked a little guilty and frowned. "I'm sorry. I was just excited for you to be yourself for a night,"

Edward smiled weakly. "I know and you know I love you both. It's just that in a place like this in Oxford there is a hierarchy in a hierarchy in a hierarchy,"

As much as Edward hated to say it, he really hadn't been prepared for Oxford at all. All these snobbish rich men and women had been bought up from birth on which wine to choose with what dish and how to eat and use your 5 different forks and knives at a formal banquet, Edward hadn't.

He had very quickly learnt that at Oxford the posher you were and the richness of your parents meant your position in the hierarchy. He was very close to the bottom.

But it was also mattered how intelligent you were and your general attitudes, including how many members of the opposite sex you slept with. Edward was helped by the intelligent just not the sex part.

And the biggest thing that Edward wasn't a fan of was that scholarship kids were instantly at the bottom of the hierarchy and it was always best to keep it a secret as long as a person could. And definitely don't tell anyone you're a gay scholarship kid.

The only thing that protected gay students at Oxford were how much money their parents had, how their parents were and how much money your parents sent the conservative party a year.

Edward had almost had a heart attack when he discovered that little truth.

"Please come," Ivy said. "Even if you aren't going to get some dick tonight. I certainly need some so I need a wingman,"

Edward smiled because he really did love Oxford, he loved Ivy and he did enjoy the parties because a lot of the rich, snobbish men seriously knew how to dress up nicely.

They were seriously fit.

"Fine I'll go," Edward said grinning.

"Excellent," Joanna shouted as her and Ivy tackled him to the ground in a hug.

And Edward had to admit he was looking forward to this party a lot more than he ever wanted to admit.

CHAPTER 3
10th March 2023
Oxford, England

As Finn stood at a very large wooden door from the last century holding a shining silver tray of champagne glasses, he had to admit he was utterly shocked at how amazing this place was. The hall the party was in was immense.

Finn focused on all the carvings of war heroes, medieval characters and horses on the huge brown wooden walls that stretched tens upon tens of metres up into the ceiling. He couldn't even see the ceiling's full height, it was so huge, but the chandelier was beautiful and the wooden carving around it created a very interesting shadow effect.

Finn wasn't sure what it was called, he hadn't covered it in his degree but it was impressive as hell and definitely something he needed to remember for the future.

He was even more impressed with all the

hundreds upon hundreds of people jammed into the huge hall. There were some insanely rich men and women slowly circulating through the crowds with their diamonds, their silk dresses and suits and million-pound watches.

Finn couldn't believe that people actually walked round wearing stuff like that but he could see it. And this was Oxford, a city he liked to call the *city of the rich, educated and snobbish.*

Finn focused on a large group of insanely new sexy men in tight-fitting black suits that just had to be tailor-made judging by how they were leaving little to the imagination, with their sexy muscles, biceps and six-packs.

If he had known there were going to be so many Greek Gods and GQ models studying here, he could have tried harder at applying for Oxford. The men here were to die for.

Finn forced himself to focus on the girls as he felt his wayward parts press firmly against his tailor-made and expensive trousers. The last thing he needed as a *servant* (not a title he liked) was to be caught getting horny about the students that were the same age as him.

He nodded to Joanna as she went through the crowd effortlessly smiling and giving the students and sponsors some kind of little pigs-in-blankets finger food. It was nice and Finn was glad to have a friend here with him.

The air smelt amazing with hints of sausages,

earthy aftershave and manly musk that made the taste of summer barbeques with his family form on his tongue. He loved his family and he couldn't believe he was privileged enough to work an event at Oxford University.

"Excuse me," a young woman said wearing a long very expensive black dress. "You might want to go somewhere else a little public,"

Finn had no idea what she was talking about until she noticed the really hot group of men he had been checking over earlier was looking at him and laughing.

Finn realised he had forgotten about his very tasteful and stylish pink hair. He just hadn't given it a second thought until now because it was just a part of him.

The young woman leant a little closer. "I know none of the wait staff go to Oxford but you aren't rich, you aren't respected and that doesn't give gay men a lot of power here,"

"What you saying?" Finn asked wanting a straight answer.

"Tell Mathew that there is a problem with your hair and he will understand. In fact I'm surprised he had you on the entrance at all," the young woman said before walking off.

Finn just stood there for a moment because he got the impression that Matt, the guy that organised the wait staff, was a good guy and that the young woman was trying to be nice, but it was such a weird thing to say.

He noticed Matt was just coming through the large entrance now so he went over to the giant of a man in a very attractive business suit and smiled.

"Apparently there is a problem with my hair," Finn said trying to sound like it was okay.

Matt rolled his eyes. "I am so sorry about that. Honestly I put you on the entrance because I want to show these snobs that gays do exist, they're okay and they aren't something to be laughed at,"

"Thanks?"

"Seriously. Go back to the entrance and if anyone questions you. Send them to me immediately,"

"Thank you I appreciate it *mate,*" Finn said.

Finn liked it as Matt went away laughing about him being deliberately common in a place like this and he went out to stand by the entrance, giving people their free glass of champagne as they came in and he noticed the large group of men were still smiling at him.

He didn't care. He was gay, happy and he loved his life. And most importantly he was working and living in the city he had always wanted to work since he was a little boy.

This really was the city of dreaming spires and-

Jesus Christ.

Finn just stopped as he focused on the back of the line coming into the hall was the hottest, sexiest, most stunning man he had ever seen. It was a shame he was walking in with a woman on his arm but he was sexy as hell.

Finn loved the Hottie's extremely slim, fit and perfectly bangable body that was almost showcased in a tailor-made navy blue suit that showed off his slight muscles and great-looking legs perfectly.

He couldn't get over the Hottie's perfectly model-like face and those deep sapphire eyes were like shards of lights that Finn just wanted to stare at for the rest of the night. He was so cute.

Finn forced himself not to react but that was impossible as his hands turned sweaty, even more sweat rolled down his back and his knees felt like they were going to collapse at any moment.

The Hottie was beyond god-like.

Finn couldn't believe he was about to give a glass of champagne to a god. This was definitely the city of dreaming spires.

Or to Finn, certainly more like the city of dreaming hot gods.

CHAPTER 4
10th March 2023
Oxford, England

Edward couldn't believe how excited he was standing in the rather short line with Ivy in a pretty little blue dress. He had always loved these parties where he could see his friends, secretly see hot men in their tight suits and he got to have great discussions with former members of the university.

The architecture of the hallway they were waiting in was huge, ancient and so amazingly detailed that Edward was surprised someone would actually have the patience for such things. It looked like someone had hand-carved little swords and heads into the brown wood of the hallway. He never could have done such a thing.

The rich smell of musk, rich earthy aftershaves and sweet flora perfumes made Edward smile and he was really looking forward to tonight. It was going to be a lot of fun and judging by the tight suits everyone else was wearing, he was hardly going to suffer from a lack of hot men.

As the line moved forward a little he felt a gentle hand tap his shoulder and him and Ivy turned round and he shook hands with her friends Alexander, Johnathan and Mathew the Third.

Edward couldn't deny they looked great in their tight white suits that highlighted their insanely fit and muscular bodies but they were definitely Oxford boys. Edward knew they wouldn't survive a moment in a public school and they certainly wouldn't last longer than five minutes on the cold mean streets of anywhere normal.

But they were nice, a laugh and Edward really did like them. The benefits of Claire dating Albert.

"How did your tuition Group go today?" Mathew asked.

Edward smiled and looked at Alex. "It went alright. The lecturer could have finished about ten minutes before the end but he loved talking. What about yours?"

Mathew shook his head. "I do not understand how after being at Oxford for three years you do not know how to speak English. It is *what about your group?* Not what about yours?"

Edward looked at Ivy because she had mentioned plenty of times how much she wanted to drag Mathew out onto the streets herself, but they both forced themselves not to laugh. He fully intended to do that later.

"However, I must confess talking to Ivo and Benaim about Liberal Arts is a useless endeavour,"

"Sorry the line's moving," Edward said grabbing Ivy and moving along.

Johnathan came up to join him. "Sorry about that, you know how many of these people are stuck so far up their own asses, they don't know how to talk normally,"

Edward laughed. "John you don't know how to talk normally?"

"That is the most outlandish idea I have ever had the misfortune of hearing," Johnathan said grinning.

"See you later *Johnathan*," Edward said.

"Bye,"

Edward gave his and Ivy's name to the poor soul on the door that looked half scared and half in awe of all the money flowing past him. Edward knew the feeling well and that was part of the culture shock of Oxford.

Money was everywhere.

"Let's grab a glass, shall we? Then mommy needs to find some dick," Ivy said.

"You are so common at times," Edward said allowing her to drag him elegantly through the crowds.

"And you love me for it,"

Edward shook his head as he neared the poor man in charge of handing out the glasses of champagne. And Edward just stopped.

Ivy almost tripped over but Edward didn't care.

All he could do was focus on the short man with beautiful, lustrous, silky smooth pink hair handing out the drinks. He was incredible and Edward couldn't believe how tasteful and stylish the man's pink hair was. He never would have been brave enough to dye his hair pink.

Of any shade.

Edward just stared at the cute, insanely divine man in his little waiter's outfit that showed how slim he was without any signs of fat or anything. The soft, lightly pink hair framed the waiter's incredibly handsome face that was so smooth and cute with his little nose, stunning eyes and beautiful smile.

That was looking straight at him.

Edward didn't know what to do but he knew he wanted to move closer to the waiter. He just couldn't. His body wasn't moving and that was okay.

"Hey," Ivy said.

Edward forced himself to look away from her and after a moment he smiled at Ivy and he could tell that she knew something was off. Then she looked at the waiter man and laughed.

Ivy came very close to his ear. "Just remember the non-horny you wouldn't want to be all over him in public. There is an exit by the stairs that lovers use to escape,"

Edward kissed her on the cheek. "Thank you,"

"Now I just need to find my own dick because I am not allowing myself to be outdone by the likes of you. My shy little best friend,"

Edward laughed and gently pushed her away and he was determined to get a drink from the most beautiful man he had ever seen.

But as he went over to the god in the waiter's uniform he couldn't help but feel his anxiety increased and his fears about being discovered only multiplied.

He was a great Oxford student but he was still the scholarship kid that didn't have rich parents, money to burn and money to donate to political parties he hated.

But Edward forced those fears away because after three years of being here and having fear in the back of his mind, he just wanted one night of freedom.

And one night of being gay with the god in the waiter's uniform.

FALLING FOR OXFORD

CHAPTER 5
10th March 2023
Oxford, England

After two hours of working, Finn had honestly expected the thrill of being at an Oxford party would have worn off but he was really glad that it hadn't. And he was even more impressed that the Hottie was slowly coming over to him.

As the chatting, laughing and live classical music in the background changed to something Finn didn't care about, he just focused on the sexy Hottie gliding through the crowd towards him. He had no idea a man could be so elegant, perfect and hot just by walking.

But the Hottie was like a walking piece of art with his beauty, elegance and just sheer authority of… normality. Finn hadn't realised that until now but he really liked that about this Hottie.

Everyone else about in this party definitely seemed to give the authority of apparently being better than everyone else, but not Him, not the divine Hottie walking towards him.

"Um hi," the Hottie said.

Finn wanted to laugh because it was sweet seeing how the Hottie was sweating, nervous and clearly didn't do this often.

"I'm, um, Edward and I don't remember seeing you before," the Hottie said not wanting Finn to know how nervous he was. "And I was just wondering if you were new here,"

Finn laughed. "You don't do this often do you? Or you are an Oxford man, do you pick up people often?"

Finn had no idea if anything he had just said was true but that was the advantage of being on the wait staff, it allowed him to watch, learn and see how people reacted to each other.

"No I never actually pick up people at parties," Edward said knowing how the wait staff watched them. "But you still haven't answered my question,"

Finn looked around to make sure no one was watching in case Matt or another senior Waiter wanted him to do less chatting and more working. Thankfully no one was watching at all.

"Yes I just moved to the area today and I had forgotten I signed up for this event to work. It seems fun, interesting and, do you like these parties?"

Finn didn't know why Edward looked a little uncomfortable but he had been gay for way too long not to know when something was off or something wasn't quite right.

"Are you one of those men smiling at me earlier?

And this is a case of *this guy must be gay so let's laugh at him?* Or did you draw the short card and you have to talk to me as a hazing thing,"

Finn liked it how Edward looked like he was about to die and he wanted the ground to swallow him whole, he looked so cute, sweet and vulnerable that Finn really wanted to hug him. But he forced himself not to.

"No no no," Edward said. "Honest it isn't that at all. I actually, I actually really like your hair. It's, you know, cute,"

Finn grinned as he understood that Edward liked him or at least found him mildly attractive and he simply wasn't comfortable talking about this sort of stuff in person. Or maybe not comfortable in front of the other Oxford lads.

"You're pretty cute too," Finn said wanting to see where this went.

Edward finally picked up a glass of champagne and Finn was glad it was at the exact right moment as a female member of the senior wait staff frowned at him, she probably thought he wasn't working. Finn would be glad when she retired or something.

"Hey," Edward said, "is there any chance you wanted to go somewhere more private and comfortable. Not for adult stuff I promise,"

Finn nodded subtly as a large group of young women walked by. The last thing he wanted was for the women to think Edward was talking to someone as low as him. Finn had watched enough tonight to sort of understand the class dynamic here.

"Great there's a staircase down by the exit. Meet me there in half an hour if you can," Edward said grinning like a little schoolboy.

Finn felt his throat go dry so all he could do was nod and he realised that he had basically just setup a date with an extremely hot Oxford boy who seemed sweet, kind and just normal in a sea of snobbishness.

And Finn's wayward parts flared to life again he couldn't believe how excited he was.

He saw Joanna and Matt talking so he subtly glided through the crowd (not as beautifully as Edward) and he smiled at them.

"Let me guess," Matt said, "you picked up an Oxford boy and you want to head off earlier,"

Finn was shocked that Matt knew that and he had no idea what had happened or how he could possibly imply that. He was perfectly professional on the job.

Matt grinned. "How do you think I met my husband? Go on I always get three extra staff members just in case this happens. Have fun and use protection,"

Finn almost died as Matt said something so common and unrefined in the middle of an Oxford party but Finn thanked him and quickly hurried off.

He had to make sure he looked his best for his private date.

But first he actually needed to find the exit and the staircase.

CHAPTER 6
10th March 2023
Oxford, England

Edward was so nervous as he went down the long corridor towards the exit and the staff-only metal staircase next to it. Edward couldn't deny that the corridor was a little different to the other ones in this area of the college, with its bright white walls, polished light wooden floors and bright chandelier lights overhead.

It was all a little too clinical for his liking but Edward just wanted to see that hot beautiful man he had been talking to earlier. Edward was almost embarrassed that he hadn't even asked the man's name.

Edward was surprised he had been that rude, if Oxford had taught him anything it was that being polite was the most British thing a person could do, and that all started by finding out what a person's name was. Edward really didn't know what other things that beautiful man had made him forget.

He had made sure to say goodnight to Ivy, Claire and all the other rich snobbish men they were hanging around. They had joked he was a lightweight and that wasn't surprising for a scholarship kid but Edward just laughed *with* them.

The joke was on them because whilst they were being their snobbish selves. Edward was really looking forward to actually being a *person*, a real one with a beautiful man. Something he hadn't done for a long, long time.

Edward smiled as a long line of waitresses came out of the kitchen area that had its own golden door and when they were all gone he started going down the long spiral staircase that had been there since the college was founded back in the 1200s.

He had already seen plenty of hot men come down here with women attached to their arms, but Edward couldn't help but feel like he was going to get caught.

When he got to the bottom he forced those feelings away and stepped out into the icy cold night that made him shiver a little. Edward had never been down here before so he was a little surprised that he was in the middle of a large garden, with massive oak trees to his left, a ton of bushes to his right and nothing but an empty field of grass in front of him.

He had no idea if normally men and women went for the bushes or trees to secretly make love to each other. He was so new to this and now he wished he had listened to Albert and his snobbish friends more about their sexual conquests so he would know what to do about now.

Even that rich and posh snobs like that never wanted to get dirty or even do so something as "common" as sex outdoors. Edward just grinned to himself because those rich men really didn't know what they were missing.

"Hi,"

Edward went over to the trees as he saw the beautiful man's stylish pink hair stand out against the darkness as he leant against a tree. Edward bit his lower lip at how hot and perfect and sexy the man looked.

He really liked it when the beautiful man threw his arms around Edward's neck and Edward pulled him close.

Then Edward stopped and gently pushed the beautiful man round to the other side of the trees so no one could see them. The beautiful man came closer to kiss him but Edward stopped him.

"Um I'm sorry. I haven't, you know I haven't done this for a while and I don't even know your name," Edward said.

The beautiful man laughed and hugged Edward. He loved the feeling of the beautiful man's warm, soft, wonderful body against his.

"It's okay, truly. I'm Finn and I sort of figured you never do this," he said liking their bodies against each other. "And that's okay, I'm a little rusty myself to be honest,"

Edward was so glad to hear that, he would have so wanted to die of embarrassment if Finn (a beautiful name to suit such a perfect man) was a sex expert or something.

Edward gently brushed Finn's wonderful pink hair and he was so impressed. He would have loved to have the confidence to dye his hair, wear a little pink or just do something, anything to subtly tell the world that he was gay.

"You're beautiful," Edward said realising how corny it sounded.

Finn let out another great laugh and Edward instantly knew he was never ever going to get tired of it.

Finn bit his lower lip. "Hey I don't normally do this either, and you seem newer than me. When was the last time you just spend a night talking to a gay guy? No kissing, no sex, no nothing. Just talking and being gay,"

Edward felt an intense wave of emotion wash over him. He hadn't realised until now just how badly, how desperately, how much he longed for something just as simple as that. He hadn't managed to find many gay people at Oxford and he was sure he wouldn't have spoken to them anyway because of his fear.

But right now he was hugging a very hot man that wasn't connected to the university, wasn't connected to his friends and most importantly he wasn't connected to the rich snobs that wouldn't like a gay scholarship kid.

Edward seriously never ever wanted this night to end.

"Let's go," Edward said.

CHAPTER 7
10th March 2023
Oxford, England

Finn was flat out amazed about how damn lucky he was to be walking hand in hand with such a divine sexy god of a man, as the two of them went along a narrow little concrete path he hadn't known existed but he was glad that Edward knew perfectly.

He was really impressed that there was a massive, perfectly tailored field of thick green grass to their right, and there was a little river to their left that was normally used for punting and other water activities that both the university students and tourists used plenty on warm summer days. It was great.

Finn liked looking into the cool calmness of the shallow water as it flowed down river with little pieces of leaves, twigs and other things he couldn't quite see in the darkness. There was the odd duck and their family swimming about and they were quacking loudly to each other.

A small gust of cold wind howled through the trees next to the river and Finn liked how the moonlight reflected gently off the water and illuminated Edward's great body, and Finn so badly wanted to kiss him, love him and just make out like horny teenagers but he could sort of guess that Edward wouldn't be comfortable with that just yet.

That was okay.

Finn loved how Edward smelt of earthy aftershave, manly musk and just perfection. He almost couldn't believe that he was in the presence of such a hot man but he knew he was and this was beyond perfect.

The incoming light from distant houses allowed Finn to see Edward's handsome face and he just stopped them both and enjoyed the moment together. There was no one about, no other sound than the quacking of the ducks and the air might have been icy but he didn't care as Edward's arms tightly wrapped round him.

Finn rested his head against Edward's wonderfully manly chest and listened to the beating of his heart. It was calming, relaxing and regular, and this just felt so natural and right.

It didn't feel forced like it had with boys from the past. It didn't feel scary or nervous like it had before, and it certainly didn't make Finn feel like anything bad was going to happen.

Because he just sort of knew that Edward liked him, found him attractive and he really felt that

Edward would always protect him no matter what happened now or in the future.

Edward gently ran his fingers through Finn's hair making him smile. "Tell me about yourself then,"

"Not really much to tell. Me and my two best friends moved into a house earlier today after close to a year of planning and talking about it, on the outskirts of the city. We've always loved Oxford and we wanted to live here,"

Finn loved it how Edward grinned at his answer like it was a joke.

"Don't mock me," Finn said pushing their bodies against each other.

"No, it's just that. You sound like you *really* like Oxford, why?"

Finn forced himself not to kiss Edward so he started to walk on and Edward quickly followed.

"Because it's just such a beautiful city. The buildings, the history and the nightlife, so I sort of had the little idea of maybe I could get a boyfriend here whilst I worked and lived here,"

Edward pulled Finn close as they went along the path. "That's working out for you so far. You've landed a guy on your first night, it's taken me three years,"

Finn almost stopped dead in his tracks. Edward had to be flat out lying about that, how the hell could such a hot beautiful man not have anyone interested in him for three years?

"You doubt me?"

Finn gasped. He hadn't meant to make that too obvious. "No it's just that you look amazing and I just don't understand how a guy like you doesn't get someone interested,"

"Truth is I'm a scholarship kid, and how much do you know about the hierarchies within Oxford?"

Finn nodded. He had read a lot about Oxford when he was younger and when he was applying to a bunch of universities and it was mainly the classist bullshit that made him decide not to go for his interview. He had done great on the entry tests but ultimately he wanted a university that would accept him wholeheartedly.

Not only accept him because it was a "proper" thing to do in these modern times.

Thankfully he had found that in Kent University, he had met Joanna and Eli and he had seriously never looked back at all. Oxford might have been his home now but it certainly never ever would have been his university city.

It just wasn't right for him, so Finn told Edward all that.

"I never could have done what you did," Edward said. "That's amazing and you really are quite courageous but I've always wanted Oxford,"

"It sounds like you're doing great,"

Finn was surprised when Edward just stopped and weakly smiled at him. "What's wrong?"

"What's it like to, you know, have a boyfriend?" Edward asked. "I know it sounds pathetic but I had some relationships in sixth form, but you know school relationships are different from real ones. And I've never dated since,"

Finn felt sorry for Edward. It was clear that he loved Oxford, he loved his studies and he never would have changed it for the world but it was clear that he had missed out on relationships. Finn had had at least three boyfriends at university and they had all been hot, passion and tender but they had mostly failed for different reasons that thankfully weren't to do with him.

But despite the heartbreak after each one, Finn still wouldn't have traded in those relationships for the world, because they were sensational whilst they lasted.

Finn went close to Edward and hugged him tight. "Relationships are complex, passionate and very hot but ultimately they come down to two people being attracted to each other and wanting to see if they have things in common past their attraction,"

Edward looked at the ground. "I would like, um, like to try that,"

Finn laughed. "Are you going ask me to out properly?"

Edward stood up perfectly straight and Finn gasped as he looked so divine, sexy and just amazing in the moonlight. "Yes I am. Give me your phone number and you and he are going on a proper date next week,"

They exchanged phone numbers and Finn gave

Edward a tender kiss on the cheek and he couldn't wait until next week.

CHAPTER 8
11th March 2023
Oxford, England

Edward was actually really surprised as he sat on a long row of ancient wooden benches and tables for breakfast that he was one of the only people in the huge eating hall.

Normally on most weekday mornings he could barely hear himself think or hear Claire or Ivy or whoever else was sitting right next to him, but today was weird. He was the only person sitting on his huge row of tables and on the two rows, there were only small clusters of first years that clearly hadn't gone to the party last night.

Edward really didn't care because it meant he could sit right in front of the ancient stained-glass window of some religious figure he couldn't have cared less about. Yet he did enjoy looking at the bright purple, pink and blue shards of glass that allowed the dim sunlight to shine through even on a cold day like today.

It was so beautiful to see and it was little reasons like this why Edward loved Oxford. It had the most amazing architecture.

Edward was about to tuck into his sterling silver bowl filled with oatmeal made from milk with from an Alpine cow, oats from the tops of Italian mountains and rich fresh berries from the deepest darkest corners of South America, when he heard his two best friends thundering towards him. Then they slowed down thankfully.

"So?" Claire and Ivy said as one as they sat down opposite him wearing a white blouse, black trousers and black high heels each.

Edward had no idea how the two women managed to walk in high heels after the party and with a hangover. He had asked before and it was apparently a skill but Edward thought it was a lot more luck than that.

"So what?" Edward asked with a grin.

"Iv told me later that you met a man," Claire said making sure no one was looking at them, and Edward was more than grateful the sheer silence of the eating hall still wasn't enough to make Claire easy to hear.

Edward grinned and leant closer. "His name was Finn, he doesn't come here and he actually lives in a house with his two best friends on the outskirts. We're seeing each other again next week,"

Ivy nodded and Edward smiled as he realised she was scheming yet again.

"That could actually be very useful to us. If your boyfriend has a house away from this place then that would be great for escapism. I know a lot of students who would enjoy that,"

"Really?" Claire said waving at Albert as he entered the hall.

"Oh yes," Ivy said, "I know of at least twenty students that would love to escape Oxford University and its ever-watchful eyes. We could charge per hour for that escape and we could be rich,"

"I am not letting you rent out my boyfriend's house,"

Claire grinned. "Dating already?"

Edward wanted to say more but then Albert sat down right next to him and gave him a firm handshake. Edward couldn't deny Albert looked great in his jeans, shirt and shoes but he was nothing compared to Finn.

"Wherever did you go last night?" Albert asked. "We were having a lot of fun waltzing with the women and making fun of the first years,"

Edward weakly smiled. "I simply wanted to walk outside and I was talking to a girl. One of the waitresses,"

Edward hated lying but this was the way it just had to be for another two months until he had his results and he could leave this place, as much as he loved it.

"Good for you," Albert said, "but you didn't meet that queer boy out there did you? You know the boy with that outlandish and disgraceful hair colour,"

Edward so badly wanted to say something, stand up for what was right but he couldn't. He was a coward and this was the price of getting into Oxford, it had worked for the past three years so two more months couldn't hurt. Surely?

"No I didn't but I would have stayed away from him anyway," Edward said, hating himself for the lie.

"Actually," Ivy said, "I saw him with a girl too. Maybe that so-called *disgraceful* boy isn't gay after all. Maybe he's bi or something, and there isn't anything wrong with that is there?"

Edward really did love Ivy at times. "I agree with Ivy and it's good that the man feels free to express himself. And come on, the basis of Oxford is improving the world through education and making the world a better place,"

Albert laughed and looked at Edward's food. "I am so glad you scholarship kids are finally learning the meaning of good food,"

Claire just looked at him. "Babe, I am a scholarship kid too,"

Edward noticed that Albert looked like he hated to be reminded of that but then he smiled and blew her a kiss.

"Anyway me and the *real* men, are going to the centre later on for some shopping, punting and other things. Did you care to join us?"

As much as Edward didn't want to spend more time with someone like Albert and his so-called friends, he did want to make sure Claire and Ivy were okay and it was all part of the social protection Ivy had so carefully crafted for them. And it would be fun to go out today and just do something to keep his mind off the hot sexy man he had met last night.

Well until they met again next week for another lovely evening.

CHAPTER 9
11th March 2023
Oxford, England

Finn was so pleased with himself as he finally sorted out getting all his clothes out of the mountain of plastic boxes in the middle of the living room. He had already put them away and now he really wanted to bring the space alive with a little interior designing.

He sat on one of the plastic boxes and pressed his back into the very uncomfortable and cold mountain of boxes, and focused on the large white walls around him. They were all his canvases so now he just had to make sure he used them correctly, to their full potential and to make sure they were a reflection of three of them.

The living room still smelt of bleach, cleaning chemicals and a vanilla candle that Eli had burnt last night when they were out, and Finn was still reeling from what had happened. It was so amazing that he was now sort of dating an Oxford man, a hot, sexy, intelligent man that was beyond perfect.

Finn still wasn't sure how he had controlled himself when they parted ways. He had wanted so badly to just kiss Edward's soft, posh lips that looked like they belonged to a god or model, but he hadn't wanted to rush Edward into anything.

It was clear that Edward wanted to take things slow and Finn was fine about that, and it just made the moment when they did kiss even more special.

But he so badly wanted to see Edward again.

"Morning lucky man," Joanna said wearing a very thin black dressing gown. "And no before you ask you are the only one of us that got lucky last night,"

"Speak for yourself," Eli said coming into the living room behind her in only a white t-shirt and black boxers that left nothing to the imagination. "I met a girl last night and she was great,"

"Hookup or maybe future girlfriend?" Finn asked.

Eli pretended to look offended. "I am nothing short of a gentleman but this girl was really interesting, great in bed and she was nice. I just didn't feel a spark with her,"

"Fair enough," Finn said.

He watched Joanna and Eli take out their fold-up camping chairs and he forced himself not to laugh. He knew they were poor young people when they could afford a house and the first few months of mortgage payments but they had no money to get furniture.

"What you thinking then interior designer?" Joanna said getting their coffee machine out of a plastic box.

Finn smiled. "Well the living room is a communal space and this is where we're going to have guests and more. So it needs to reflect our personalities but not so much that it is off-putting to guests. Then it is our bedrooms that we really can go to town with,"

Joanna nodded as she got water. "Okay fair enough,"

Eli leant forward. "And I'm interested in history and so's Joanna. Is that allowed in the living room?"

"Of course," Finn said, "and we are in Oxford after all. I'm thinking of a kind of old world finish to the living room. So a lot of dark wooden tones, we re-vanish the floors to make sure they're extra dark and then we can bring in little ancient things and antiques to give the space some extra depth,"

Eli laughed. "And that is why everyone you are the First Class student and we only got high 2:1s,"

Finn took a mocking bow. "Thank you, thank you very much,"

Joanna laughed as she came back in and popped the coffee machine on and just grinned at Finn.

"You want to know who the man was last night?" Finn said knowing that this was going to happen at some point and considering they were all going to be spending the day together doing unpacking he supposed it was best to just get it over with.

"Yep," Eli said.

"Fine, his name is Edward Lords. A scholarship kid that is so hot, so perfect and so god-like. He seems perfectly normal for an Oxford student and he's nice and sweet and whenever I think about him my stomach fills with butterflies,"

"Ah that's so sweet," Joanna said. "When are you seeing him again?"

Finn rolled his eyes. The very last thing he was ever going to do was tell Eli and Joanna when and where they were going out together. He was just grateful they hadn't set a date yet.

"We're meeting next week at some point. We're going to phone or text each other later about it but you two would love him," Finn said not *knowing* if that was true but he certainly felt it.

Joanna looked at Eli. "If you two ever want a date round here. We could make ourselves disappear?"

Finn laughed. "Liars. The last time you did that you magically turned up for dinner and interrogated my boyfriend all evening because, what was it, oh yeah your *film* was cancelled,"

Joanna poured them all a cup of coffee as they all laughed about that evening. As much as Finn was never going to admit it, it had actually made him love his best friends even more. That evening had shown him exactly how much they loved, cared and treasured him.

And he certainly treasured them now.

But all he knew was that it was going to be a very long, torturous week until he could see the beautiful man he really liked again.

CHAPTER 10
15th March 2023
Oxford, England

Over the past four days, Edward had flat out loved texting, calling and just being in their little secret relationship. He couldn't believe how amazing it felt to connect, talk and just start getting to know an utterly divine angelic man that would never ever judge him for being gay at Oxford.

It was completely incredible.

The Six Candles was a great little old-fashioned pub near to the heart of Oxford. Edward had always liked coming here with his friends after exams in his first and second year because of its cheap prices, ancient wooden beams and plain while walls that really made the place look like it was from the last century.

Edward sat at a small square wooden table near the back of the pub on the top floor where the lighting wasn't so good, but if Finn asked why he was here he would simply say the lighting was romantic. It wasn't a complete lie, it just meant there was less chance of anyone seeing him with such a beautiful man.

The pub was loud for a Wednesday night with everyone from the old and young, posh and common and student and non-students, were laughing, chatting and shouting at their friends about what to order themselves instead of simply going to the bar themselves.

Edward really liked how the air smelt of manly musk, cheap beer and fine alcohol that he was really tempted to indulge in, but he didn't want to be drunk in front of Finn.

Just in case he did anything he might regret later on.

A moment later Edward just gasped as his wonderful angel came over to him, and Edward had never ever seen such a gorgeous man in all his life. The way Finn's tight black shirt washed over his incredible body was to die for, and his tight blue jeans left nothing to the imagination.

And Edward just wanted him.

It took Edward everything he had not to just get up, kiss Finn and do extremely adult things with him just there in the pub.

"You look, sensational," Edward said getting up and giving Finn a quick kiss on the kiss.

Finn blushed and sat down. "Thanks, you don't look so bad yourself. I've never heard of this place, what is it?"

"The Six Candles. I thought you might like it because, um, interior design whatever," Edward said.

He felt so embarrassed as he had no idea about Finn's degree subject but he was really interested in learning more, a lot more.

Edward was even more surprised when Finn actually looked like he was studying the place, like there was actually something of interest in the white walls, thick beams and just dark pub vibes. Edward had no idea what could possibly be so interesting.

"What is it?" Edward asked not understanding his interest.

"Well this is actually great you know," Finn said knowing he had no clue why he was interested, "because me and my friends are currently decorating our living room,"

Edward leant forward. "Okay what kind of design are you going for?"

"A sort of oldie world thing because my friends did history degrees at uni and I really like that sort of design. Do you know of any good antique shops?"

Edward just stared at Finn's handsome face. It was so great seeing how happy, excited and passionate Finn was about designing some living room for his friends. Edward didn't know them but they sounded like really good friends, but Edward sort of just knew that Finn was the type of amazingly nice guy that did things for people.

He was brilliant.

"Earth to Edward?"

"Oh sorry," Edward said. "I actually don't know it isn't really my thing but, you know, we could go exploring together if you want,"

"Is that okay?" Finn said leaning forward. "I just guessed you weren't too confident about being out in Oxford publicly in case one of the posh snobs from your uni sees you,"

As much as Edward hated that Finn was right and that was one of his biggest concerns, he actually didn't care. He was with a sweet, generous, adorable man and Edward had no idea why he shouldn't show Finn off to the world.

Nothing bad could happen to them and he just wanted, needed to spend more time with such a great man that was so damn cute.

"I don't care if I'm with you," Edward said, regretting it as soon as he said it.

"It's okay," Finn said laughing and Edward guessed his regret must have shown on his face. "We've been texting for days now and I think you really like me. And you know neither one of us is a dating expert,"

Edward nodded. That was certainly true. "Thanks for understanding. What do you want to drink?"

"I'm boring I know but just a Diet Coke please,"

Edward took out his phone and ordered their drinks on the app. There was no chance in hell that he was getting up to order drinks if that meant leaving

Finn and not getting to be with him for a few moments.

And Edward realised that he felt so relaxed, so calm and just like his *true* self around this angelic man. Something he hadn't felt for ages.

"Hi Finn," a woman and a man said as they came over.

Edward jumped.

He didn't know what was going on but judging by the look at Finn's face he knew actually who they were and they certainly weren't foes.

"Hi Joanna, Eli," Finn said with a massive grin. "Fancy seeing you two here out of all the bars and pubs in Oxford,"

Edward smiled at the beautiful man he was falling for. "They came to make sure I'm not going to hurt you, right?"

"Well that was a serious concern considering you know, you are a rich posh snobby Oxford boy," Joanna said. "Our words not little Finn here,"

Edward just laughed because they were clearly great friends and he was glad Finn had these people in his life.

"How about," Edward said, "if you leave us alone on this date. I will come round on Saturday and you can interrogate me as much as you want,"

Edward forced himself not to laugh at the sheer look of shock and horror at Joanna's and Eli's faces.

"You would put yourself through that?" Joanna asked.

"You're clearly important to Finn so why not?" Edward asked.

Finn got up and hugged him. "Your funeral," he said as he gave Edward a little kiss on the cheek.

CHAPTER 11
16th March 2023
Oxford, England

Finn went into a beautiful little antique shop that might have only been ten metres tall by three metres wide but it was filled with so many treasures on its dark wooden shelves that went from the floor to the ceiling.

He was really pleased to see how many little globes, little fake relics from the 18th and 19th century and there were just so many cool things here. It was even better that the shop was completely empty with only the young woman in a black dress standing behind a till.

Finn wasn't sure about the long row of ancient books on shelves in the middle of the shop but he might check them out later just in case there were any good present ideas for Joanna.

But Finn just held Edward's hand loosely as he started looking at some ancient little globes and navigation equipment at the back of the store. Holding Edward's hand just felt so right, so natural and so perfect like they had been a couple for years.

And he still couldn't believe Joanna and Eli had followed him to his date last night, but it had been fun. They had left as soon as Edward had stupidly mentioned about making to the house on Saturday (they still had so much unpacking to do) but after that Finn had just been constantly laughing, smiling and happy.

His face was still hurting and it had seriously been the best date of his life. He loved it.

"What are you looking for?" Edward asked like Finn was crazy for focusing on this stuff.

Finn didn't mind that Edward thought this was all junk or something but to Finn this was so much more and he actually wanted to try educating Edward a little.

Finn stood up perfectly straight and noticed the young woman was watching them with a large smile.

"You see all these objects," Finn said pointing to some navigation equipment from the last century that was covered in gold. "You see them as some relic knock-off. Which they are,"

Finn winked at the young woman and she silently laughed.

"But these objects add different tones, different layers of history, class and depth to a room that can be used to add or destroy a feel that I want to achieve,"

It was so cute that Edward didn't look like he understood this at all. Finn so badly wanted to kiss him.

"Think about it like this," Finn said, "you live in an Oxford dorm room in one of the ancient colleges. Everything is old with dark wooden tones, ancient pieces of art and more. If I stuck a bright white modern computer suite in there, would it look weird, off or simply out of place?"

"All of them," Edward said.

"Exactly and it would no longer look for an Oxford College, or it would no longer look like what you imagine or the effect that the designer was after,"

"Okay I think I'm starting to get it,"

Finn picked a small little golden compass covered in fake gold and ancient markings. "If you put this in your dorm room it will help deepen the old world effect that the design wanted,"

Edward nodded, and Finn looked at the young woman who was looking impressed as hell.

"Can I buy this for my boyfriend please?" Finn asked.

The young woman took the compass and went to do it on the cash register. "You're a lucky man sir,"

"I know I am," Edward said.

Finn hugged him and he so badly wanted to kiss Edward but he forced himself not to because it wasn't fair on Edward. It was great that they were in public together so he didn't want to push Edward's comfort zone too much unless he was ready for it.

Finn went over to the cash register and paid and gave the compass to Edward.

"Thanks," Edward said looking like he actually liked it. Finn was so glad about that, he had bought little gifts like that before for men that hated them.

Finn knew he was so lucky to have someone like Edward that appreciated him, his gifts and his design knowledge.

"May I ask," the young woman said, "what you were after for your project? Forgive me for assuming, but I think you came in here for a project, saw the item and bought it for your lucky boyfriend as a surprise present. Not because you came in here for it,"

Finn was impressed. This young woman was clearly a lot more knowledgeable than he gave her credit for.

"Actually," Finn said, "I want to create an oldie world effect on mine and my friend's living room,"

The young woman nodded and went over to the front of the store and pointed to a shelf of ancient fake golden artifacts that looked like they were freed from some deep dark jungle in the Amazon.

Edward nodded. "These look great,"

Finn rolled his eyes. One interior design lesson and Edward already thought himself an expert.

Finn looked down at the shelf below it and noticed there was a long line of little pots of different paints and vanishes based on different time periods.

"These effects are mainly wanted by film props,"

the young woman said. "I wanted them a lot in my film study degree. I liked working with them and they're great for making things look older than they really are,"

"I'll take them please," Finn said.

As the young woman finished up for him, Finn just looked into the stunning, beautiful eyes of the man he was so glad to be dating. Edward was so kind, understanding and he actually wanted to listen to him talk about interior design, which was certainly his other love.

That was rare to find in a man so Finn was really glad they had the rest of the day together.

But the next two days before Saturday he didn't doubt were going to be long, torturing and Finn couldn't wait to see Edward again.

FALLING FOR OXFORD

CHAPTER 12
17th March 2023
Oxford, England

Edward sat in a wonderfully warm red leather chair from the last century in one of the many common rooms in the college as he texted Finn about what he wanted to wear, bring and do to him tomorrow night. He never would have said half the things he was saying to other men but there was just something so great and special about Finn.

He felt like he really could be himself about him and that was an amazing feeling to have.

Edward liked having the common room to himself and he could easily put his feet up on the green leather poof with no one kicking him off it. All the other red leather chairs were scattered around the room and there was no one to interrupt him texting Finn.

The only bad thing about the common room was the ugly bright red wallpaper that was starting to come off the wall at the top and around the edges. It was clear as day that the common room was from the last two centuries but it was a great space for talking, drinking and just being Oxford students.

Edward hoped Claire and Ivy would turn up soon so they could tell him about what they were up to with Albert last night. It was some party apparently but wasn't too interested in the details. He only wanted to know that his two best friends were okay.

"How are you this morning?" Albert said as he walked in and Edward immediately sat up a lot straighter.

Edward subtly put his phone away. There was no way in hell he wanted Albert to see who he was texting and what he was saying in those messages.

"I'm good thank you. How was the party last night?"

"It was the most awful affair and it was filled with the most outlandish commons about women and heterosexuals. I mean it is ridiculous the belief of some students about gays and the rest of them,"

Edward didn't dare comment. He simply smiled and leant forward slightly. "What were they saying?"

Albert leant forward like they were spies talking about a matter of national security. "I was talking with a bunch of students from the more liberal colleges and they said the outlandish idea of increasing the number of gay students here,"

"No," Edward said mockingly.

"I know, can you believe it? Oxford is a world-leading institution built on the back of strong conservative men. If we allow too many of *those* people into our university they will destroy it. Destroy it I tell you,"

Edward so badly wanted to laugh but he made himself not to. Albert was talking complete crap but these were the beliefs of the all-rich and powerful in the UK.

"Good talking to you old chap," Albert said getting up as Claire and Ivy walked in wearing matching blue dresses.

Claire gave her boyfriend a long, tender kiss and Albert left. Edward gestured them to sit down and he moved his chair closer to them.

"Do you actually love him?" Edward asked.

Claire smiled. "Sort of. I love you both more, but Albert is just on top of the hierarchy. And I date him to protect you too,"

Edward looked at Claire. "What do you mean protect us?"

"She means," Ivy said frowning," that you and me are easy pickings for the bullying crowd. There aren't that many at Oxford but you know what Albert is like. If you aren't conservative and rich you are nothing,"

Claire took Edward's hand. "You're too great of a friend for me to see you get hurt so I yeah I date something like Albert to protect you. It is fun and-"

Edward waved her silent and just hugged her. "I love you Claire but you don't have to do anything for me. You're my friend and whatever happens I will stand up for both of you no matter who you're dating,"

Edward liked it how Ivy and Claire hugged him tight and he couldn't believe that Claire would do such a thing just to protect him because he was a poor little nerd in a sea of stupidly rich and snobbish students.

"How about we go punting today?" Ivy asked.

"As long as Edward's back for his date," Claire said.

Edward couldn't help but grin with excitement. He was so looking forward to seeing Finn again tonight. He would have loved Claire and Ivy to meet him but he wasn't sure if *he* was ready for that.

He really, really liked Finn but the idea of his Oxford and Finn-related worlds meeting was scary as hell.

Edward winked at Claire. "What's the scheme today?"

"I am so glad you asked," Ivy said. "There is a new punter starting today called Ben and he is the son of a shipping Mogul for a father, but his mother is a legendary clinical psychologist,"

"You want me to form a new contact," Edward said.

"No I want us all to form a new contact. We become friends with him and overtime we start forming a relationship with his mother too. And according to my sources he is very nice on the eyes as well,"

"And you still need dick from a week ago," Edward said.

"Exactly," Ivy said.

Edward just laughed and shook his head. It was so typical of Ivy to come up with a plan to help them get a new friend, form a new contact and it was extremely typical of her to have sources and informants.

Sometimes Edward really didn't know how dangerous Ivy was to the people that crossed her. Thankfully he knew he would never ever have to find out personally.

CHAPTER 13
18th March 2023
Oxford, England

Finn was so glad it had only taken him just over a week of living in Oxford for him to find a little job in an office that he could start on Monday, so he could finally start earning some cash for his lifestyle in his new city.

But as he stood in the middle of the living room, he just wasn't sure that the massive fluffy black throw he had put over the last six plastic boxes was very convincing. He wasn't sure if it would show him up as a mess to Edward or if he wouldn't notice they were still unpacking.

Finn had really tried to finish unpacking today but Joanna and Eli had been unpacking their own things, so Finn had been left alone to unpack their random six plastic boxes of utter crap that their parents had gifted them, because as his mother had said *you never know when you might need it.*

Finn was very sure he wasn't going to need a robot vacuum cleaner that was broken, he was sure he wasn't going to use an airfryer without the frying basket and he was fairly sure all their parents had packed up boxes of rubbish so Finn and his best friends would have to get rid of them instead of themselves.

He loved his parents but this was a little cheeky even for them.

Someone knocked at the door.

Finn couldn't believe that Edward was actually here and on time and he wasn't even changed yet. He had been way too busy focusing on everything else, making sure the living room was perfect and he hadn't even had a shower yet.

This was going to end badly.

He heard Joanna in her long black dress and Eli in his jeans and shirt rush down the stairs to the door like vultures to get to Edward.

Finn really wanted to rush upstairs but he was frozen. This was the first time in years he had let a man into his home, his space, his private area.

The living room was okay with its very rich, dark floors that the three of them had vanished yesterday together. Finn was really pleased with some old vanished driftwood he had found and managed to make shelves out of.

But his favourite so far had to be the vibrant baby blue walls that added a lot of lightness to the living room, but also modern, fun and calming undertones to the space too.

"Wow," Edward said. "You look great,"

Finn spun around. He couldn't look great. Edward had to be lying or mocking him.

Then Finn focused and blushed and gasped when he saw Edward had a massive bunch of red roses for him.

And Edward came over and just kissed him on the lips. Finn was shocked at how warm, refreshing and intense the kiss was. Edward's lips tasted so sweet and lustrous and velvety that he never wanted the mind-blowing kiss to stop.

This was perfect, beyond perfect.

"But I haven't changed," Finn said.

"I don't care. You look amazing to me,"

"Why don't my boyfriends say that to me?" Joanna said.

Finn was even surprised when Edward gave two little black boxes to Joanna and Edward and they both laughed as little glass bottles the size of shots were inside, with a drink Finn didn't recognise. It looked whiskey but he couldn't be sure.

"This is great mate thanks," Eli said giving Edward a hug before Joanna gave him a little kiss on the cheek.

Finn was impressed. Joanna and Eli rarely acted like this towards one of his boyfriends. He knew this was going to be a brilliant night.

Finn took Edward's smooth, soft hands in his and pulled him over to a very modern blue fabric sofa they had bought recently. It was barely big enough for two people but Finn didn't mind being so close to Edward that their bodies were tightly against each other.

And Finn couldn't deny it did add in a certain level of coziness to the living room, which would work great with some of the larger, less cozy plans he had for the space.

"How was punting?" Finn asked as they sat down, knowing that Edward had mentioned it in a text earlier.

"It was great thanks. A lot of fun with our new guide Ben who Ivy is currently *educating* in the ways of the lower classes in his bedroom. He's a great guy and I'm glad we might be friends with him,"

Finn was looking forward to meeting this Ivy woman at some point, she sounded a little scheming but fun, normal and a real laugh.

Finn shook his head and smiled as Joanna and Eli downed their whiskey bottles and then they pulled over their camping chairs.

"It isn't much. Sorry," Joanna said. "We must seem like homeless people to you,"

Finn didn't know if Joanna was being a dick on purpose or something but he smiled as Edward slowly shook his head.

"No, believe me you don't. I'm a scholarship kid and this room is actually better than when my parents divorced and my mother took me and my siblings in,"

Finn hugged Edward tight, loving the feeling of

each muscle move as he talked and moved.

"Me and my siblings were lucky to have anything of our own as kids. I remember we only have my mother's desk as a coffee table, dining table and a place to do our homework,"

Finn never knew that.

"My mother used her desk to make fake things to pawn and sell to others. It all got better over time and by the time I started sixth form I could have my own clothes, but it was rough. So no Joanna, I will never judge you to moving into a brand-new house without much of anything,"

Finn kissed him without thinking. That had to be one of the sweetest things he had ever heard and it actually made him like Edward even more.

"Thank God then," Eli said getting up ripping the black throw off the six plastic boxes.

Finn laughed as he watched Eli fold it up and use it as a cushion. "My camping chair is uncomfortable,"

"Let's swap," Edward said.

Finn just grinned as his stomach filled with butterflies because Edward was a really sweet man that was caring, thoughtful and so perfect.

Finn never wanted this moment to end.

Joanna rolled her eyes. "We better order a pizza or whatever because I can't cook and I don't feel like our resident chef wants to take his eyes off you for a moment,"

Finn blushed and Joanna wasn't wrong. If cooking meant he had to look away from Edward for a single moment then he really didn't want to do it.

"Pizza sounds great," Edward said kissing Finn again.

And Finn was growing to love each kiss even more than the last. This was going to be a sensational night and Finn never wanted it to end.

Not for a single moment.

CHAPTER 14
18th March 2023
Oxford, England

Three hours later, Edward absolutely loved how beautiful, precious Finn was resting his head on his lap as the two of them just laughed, talked and enjoyed their time with Joanna and Eli. Edward was seriously impressed with what they wanted for the future, why they had wanted to come to Oxford, but most importantly Edward flat out enjoyed spending time with all of them.

Edward really understood why Finn liked them so much. Joanna and Eli were fun to be around and they really knew their stuff. And their interrogation hadn't been that bad after all.

Edward gently ran his fingers through Finn's pink hair and he just loved how soft, velvety and perfect it felt. And for a moment he realised that he didn't deserve a man as perfect, charming and fit as Finn but there was something in Finn's eyes that told him that he was wrong.

Finn really, really liked him.

As the two of them still sat on the sofa and Eli and Joanna had added more pillows and blankets to the camping chairs as the night had gone on, Edward flicked open some of their five pizza boxes and managed to find a single slice of vegan BBQ chicken still untouched.

He went to eat it but then Finn, like a cat, pulled at his arm so he carefully popped it in Finn's mouth and they smiled and laughed about it together.

Edward couldn't believe how weird and vulnerable that little thing was, but it felt great to do it. He felt so comfortable with Finn that he didn't care if he did slightly weird and loved up rubbish.

All that mattered was that he was with the boy he really, really liked.

"I need to get a boyfriend that does that," Joanna said.

Edward smiled at her. "Only so you wouldn't have to get out of bed to get breakfast,"

"True true," Joanna said. "Should we open another bottle of wine?"

Edward looked down at his feet and noticed there was still a full glass of red wine that he hadn't even touched, even though Joanna had given it to him over an hour ago. He had enjoyed the nice fruity tones coming from the rich full-bodied wine but it was strong.

Too strong.

He couldn't finish it. "No thanks, I better get back to the college soon,"

Finn got up and hugged him tight. "Stay the night, please. I want you to stay and I don't want you to go,"

Edward grinned. There wasn't anything else he would have liked more. The idea of seeing Finn's thin, sexy body naked and spread out on the bedsheets was certainly a great reason to stay but Edward knew there would be other students up and awake in the common room when he got home, and they would remember *if* he came home which was what he wanted.

If they saw him come home then no one would ask questions, no one would ask why he smelt of pizza, man musk and red wine. If he didn't return and if he was out tonight then there would be a lot of questions.

And as much as Edward just wanted to live his own life, he didn't want to lie to rich snobbish students that could easily call up their parents to cause him as much trouble as they wanted with the college heads. He had seen it happen before and he knew it would happen long after he left.

It was the way the elite worked.

Edward took Finn's hand in his and kissed it. "I promise you. We'll sleep together soon and we can spend the night together,"

He loved how Finn grinned like a little schoolboy at the idea and he loved it too. Then he realised next weekend was the perfect opportunity because it was the start of the Easter break and there was the weird but very fun Maskara Ball with an Easter theme. No one would know if he was at the Ball or not.

"Next weekend you and me. We go out, have fun and we come back here and fuck like crazy," Edward said.

Edward loved it as Finn gave him a hard, tender, passionate kiss that held so much sexual tension and so much promise of a brilliant night.

"I will hold you to that," Finn said.

Edward was about to say more when he caught Joanna and Eli smiling at him, he had completely forgotten they were there. But he would love Finn to meet Claire and Ivy, and he just had a little feeling that Finn and Ivy would seriously get on well.

Edward got up, said goodnight to Joanna and Eli and simply let Finn out of the living room. Then Edward pushed Finn up against the white wall of the hallway and gave him a real kiss.

A lover's kiss.

Edward grinned as they broke the kiss and Finn looked so damn cute as he looked shocked but really pleased.

"Meet my best friends next week," Edward said. "I want you to know me and my life and I really *really* like you,"

Finn looked like a deer in headlights for a moment before he slowly nodded and recovered. "One week today you want me to meet your best friends and have sex with you. Is that too much for you?"

Edward laughed and hugged the man he seriously liked. "I don't care anymore. I like you and that's all that matters,"

He didn't have the heart to tell Finn why he didn't want to stay today, but he was really hoping to make up for it next Saturday.

"One week," Finn said kissing Edward firmly on the lips. "I'll be counting down the hours,"

Edward laughed and left and prepared to get a bus back to the college but he certainly couldn't disagree. He couldn't wait for next Saturday because he knew it was going to be a magical, wonderful, sensational night that he was going to remember for the rest of his life.

Little did he realise he would certainly remember it but not for the reasons he expected. Or hoped for.

CHAPTER 15
25th March 2023
Oxford, England

After three hours of preparing, deciding what to wear and making sure he looked at best he was ever going to be (even under his clothes), Finn was seriously looking forward to tonight. He knew it was going to be fun with so much hot stuff going on and he was really looking forward to finally meeting Edward's best friends too.

They had been texting all week about their plans for after dinner with Claire and Ivy and Finn could tell that Edward was nervous as hell. He might have been a bottom from his texts but Finn didn't care. All he cared about was that he was finally going to see, touch and feel Edward's naked body against him.

Finn sat in a very hard wooden chair in the Devil's Child, a strange little pub on the outskirts of Oxford with jet black wooden walls, black wooden tables and lights made from skulls. He had no idea why Edward wanted to meet here but it wasn't the worse pub he had ever been in.

The entire place was packed with university students dancing, making out and eating great-looking food. Finn really liked the look of some incredibly juicy steaks with crispy chips that looked beyond sensational.

The entire place smelt of succulent meat, garlic and rosemary and another million senses that Finn couldn't name. The entire place smelt amazing.

"Claire, Ivy this is my boyfriend Finn," Edward said as Finn saw his hot as hell boyfriend in extremely tight-fitting black jeans, black shirt and black shoes.

Edward might have almost blended into the walls of the pub but Finn didn't care. He looked so sexy, hot and Finn so badly wanted to pound him right now in the middle of the pub.

Finn smiled and hugged Ivy, who was wearing a little bright red dress that made her stand out in the pub but Finn had a feeling that was all by design. And a scheme.

Then Finn hugged Claire who was wearing a very beautiful white dress that made her look like an angel in amongst the darkness of the pub.

"How can you possibly get more beautiful each time I see you?" Edward said giving Finn a little kiss.

Finn was a little surprised it wasn't as deep or passionate as they normally did, but Finn supposed that was only because Edward was shy about them being a couple in front of his Oxford friends.

"We've heard tons about you," Claire said. "You look as cute as Edward described you, but he says you're from Canterbury originally,"

Finn subtly looked at Edward as he sat down.

"What do you think is the best uni down?" Claire asked.

Finn smiled because the answer were plain as day considering there was Kent Uni then the other two unis down there weren't real universities. One was all about arts and performance and the other was all about gaming.

He still wasn't sure why someone needed a degree for gaming.

"You're both local then," Finn said knowing that only people from Kent would know something as silly as that.

"Relax about us," Ivy said. "We're all scholarship and we aren't snobs, and I'm under strict orders not to scheme tonight,"

Finn leant forward. "Coming from the woman in a bright red dress in the middle of a black place. You stand out like a candle. Who are you after?"

"Everyone," Edward said holding Finn's hand, "later on I bet you she's going to pretend to be *nice* to us and buy us drinks. That way she goes to the bar, men see her and then we never get our drinks and then we don't see her until the next afternoon,"

Finn smiled at Ivy. "How many times you done that?"

"You know what they say," she said, "a hot sexy

flame cannot be held responsible for how many men she sleeps with,"

"No one says that," Claire said hugging her sister.

Finn laughed as he had a great feeling about tonight and he was going to really like spending time with Claire and Ivy. It was clear that Ivy was a bit of a wildcard but Finn was sure she had some great stories to tell.

And for them to laugh about.

"I'm going to get us drinks now," Ivy said.

"Oh no you aren't. Not alone, I actually want something to drink," Claire said following her sister.

Finn smiled and just looked at the stunning man he seriously liked.

"I'm sorry if they're a bit much but they are amazing,"

Finn shook his head and brushed his fingers through Edward's wonderfully thick hair. "They're perfect and I want to hear Ivy's stories,"

Edward moved closer and Finn loved it as he caressed his neck and he started moving fingers through his pink hair.

"I'm not responsible if you're jealous of what her past boyfriends have done to her,"

Finn moved so closer to Edward that their lips grazed each other. "You might have to show me what they've done in case I don't understand from the stories,"

"There's nothing I would love more," Edward said.

Finn went hard as they were just about to kiss.

"Edward!" a man shouted.

Edward went instantly tense, shot up like a flag like he looked like a deer in headlights. Finn watched as the man came over with two others.

They looked great in their expensive silk suits but Finn could tell these were *real* Oxford students from money and power and everything he didn't like.

"Where are you doing about to kiss *that* excuse of a man?" the man asked.

Finn stood up and went to hold Edward's hand but he moved away.

And that simple movement killed Finn inside. Why would the man he liked more than anything not want to hold his hand in crisis?

What wasn't Edward telling him?

CHAPTER 16
25th March 2023
Oxford, England

Edward flat out couldn't believe how bad, messed up and dire this situation was. He had chosen tonight because all week Albert, Ivo and Alexander had been banging on and on about how they were attending the Ball.

They weren't meant to be here. This was also the local pub where non-students were but clearly the damn bar had decided to remarket itself.

Edward didn't really want to move away from Finn but the best thing he could do was to get Albert away from the beautiful man he really liked. If Albert went away then he wouldn't say or do anything against Finn and Edward could also protect Claire and Ivy.

He just had to make sure everyone got out of this situation okay.

"I wasn't going to kiss him," Edward said firmly,

"and I wasn't having dinner with him because I noticed he was here alone and I recognised him. We were only talking,"

Albert didn't seem convinced. "I know it's dark but I saw what was happening. The idiot's a beacon with his girly hair,"

"You're wrong. I would never date a man. It's just nowhere near as good as with a woman and a man with a man isn't the Oxford way,"

Edward hated what he was saying but he had to protect Finn no matter the cost.

"The idiot's a beacon with his girly hair,"

Edward so badly wanted to hit Albert or something but he couldn't. Albert was a lot more powerful physically and within Oxford for him to do that.

Edward looked at Finn and just mouthed *Trust Me*.

"I've never seen him before," Finn said but Edward could tell the words were forced. "And come on like I would lower myself to kissing a guy like Edward,"

Edward rolled his eyes as if that was true then how did Finn know his name.

Edward hated it as Albert smiled and he simply took three steps closer to Edward until they were standing eye to eye. Albert was so close to Edward that he could feel his disgusting breath on his face.

"I knew scholarship kids were useless common scum that never deserved to be at a place like Oxford.

I will get you kicked out and when my father is in power. He will make sure you fags serve men like me,"

Edward couldn't take it.

He punched Albert square in the nose.

Albert collapsed to the ground.

Screaming like a baby.

Holding his nose.

"Help help help. You broke my nose. Help me please someone," Albert shouted.

Edward just shook his head as Albert forced himself up and he just ran away like the coward he was.

He made sure that Albert and his friends were gone before he looked at Finn at again, but he was frowning.

"You aren't my boyfriend?" Finn asked. "You don't care about us, our relationship or anything when you face a bit of trouble from your rich pompous friends?"

Edward just froze as he realised exactly what he had done both to Finn and Albert. He had completely reinforced whatever beliefs and doubts Finn secretly had about their relationship because he had never wanted it to be public.

And Edward had shown Finn why but he had completely forsaken him at the same time.

Edward hated how he had done that, and now he had just assaulted Albert, a very powerful and rich student in his college. He had to check with Claire just how powerful he really was.

"I didn't mean it,"

Finn laughed and took a few steps back. "You didn't mean a man and a man aren't right. You didn't mean you didn't like me. You didn't mean any of how you fucking invalidate our entire relationship!"

Edward so badly wanted the ground to swallow him whole.

"I liked you so damn much. I invited you into my life, you met my friends and I was going to let you do so many things to me tonight. Are you straight or something and I was just a curiosity?"

"No!" Edward shouted by mistake realising everyone was looking at him now. "I really liked you, I probably loved you but… I don't want to make enemies with my fellow students. Some of them are fixed in their ways,"

Finn shook his head. "Well you don't need to worry about that now. We are done and I'll find myself a man that actually does think a man with a man is right and I don't care about your fancy degree or whatever. Grow a backbone and stand up for what *you* think is right instead of other people,"

Edward went to grab his arm but he forced himself not to because Finn was right. Totally bloody right.

Edward was a dick and he had just done every single thing he hadn't wanted to do tonight. He hadn't wanted Albert and the others to find out, he hadn't wanted Claire and Ivy to get hurt but they would, and most importantly he flat out hadn't wanted Finn to get hurt.

Because as Edward watched him walk away Finn realised he didn't actually like Finn.

He loved him.

CHAPTER 17
28th March 2023
Oxford, England

A few days later, Finn just couldn't believe how stupid he was for allowing someone, an Oxford boy no less, into his heart and just disrespecting him so badly. It was awful, he hated himself and he really hated Oxford even more.

As Finn just laid on their little sofa against a blue wall of the living room, he realised he had always seen Oxford as the city of dreaming spires but it wasn't. It seriously wasn't. It was more like the city of evil demonic backstabbers.

All Finn wanted more than anything else in the world was a cute, sweet man that could love him, respect him and just want to be with him. Why was that so hard?

His new office job had been bad enough yesterday and today with all those silly new workers talking about their boyfriends, girlfriends and how great their lives were. Finn had no clue why they were so happy.

He wasn't.

A moment later Finn rolled his eyes as Joanna and Eli came back from shopping with large white tote bags filled with food, drinks and more cakes than Finn wanted to know about. It was great seeing them so happy, cheerful and smiling about something but Finn didn't like it.

There was nothing for him to smile about.

"And how's our little heartbroken friend?" Joanna asked.

Finn forced himself to sit up no matter how heavy, lifeless and pointless his entire body felt. Then he noticed that Eli was holding a small catalogue belonging to a high-end antique shop.

Finn grinned as he took it. He hadn't felt a paper catalogue for ages with its rough paper, fresh ink smell and heavy weight. The catalogue felt almost as heavy as his arms did.

"We thought you might want to get some ideas for the living room," Joanna said. "You know, to help take your mind off it,"

Finn frowned as she reminded him of what he was failing to forget. He had hated himself for how he had come home gotten so drunk that Joanna and Eli had come down in the morning thinking he was dead.

Even now the lingering effects of the killer hangover were still there but Finn just wanted to forget about Edward, the beautiful perfect man that he cared so much about. Clearly alcohol wasn't the answer so he had given up on that yesterday.

Joanna went over to the middle of the living room. "Come on Finn what about a massive globe here?"

Finn laughed. He had to admit he had enjoyed working on the living room for the past two days when he wasn't sulking about Edward. Everything was almost done now with his design really coming along and it was perfect.

The light baby blue walls really helped to make the space feel light, airy and modern. The dark wooden floors contrasted the walls nicely and helped to set the space up for the old world design, with the brand-new antique shelves, bookcases and other little things he got from various places gave the living room so much depth, texture and subtly all helped draw the eye towards the centre of the living room.

The place where everyone sat, ate and talked. It was the centre of the living room that was really the heart of the home.

It would have been amazing to show Edward all this but Edward just didn't care about him as much as Finn cared about him.

Eli came over and hugged him. "How are you doing?"

Finn folded his arms. "All I wanted was for him to be good to me. I wanted to be with him, support him and I didn't care if he felt we couldn't be a public thing until after his degree. But he should have told me,"

"You were good about making sure he wanted to cross lines and make the next steps," Joanna said.

"Exactly," Finn said. "It was Edward that was making us kiss, have sex and do things. I just respected him and then all of a sudden he doesn't want to do any of them,"

"Talk about mixed signs," Eli said.

Finn could only agree. It was only now he was realising just how annoyed he was, it wasn't even the fact that Edward had said they weren't boyfriends that was annoying him (well not now anyway), it was the fact that Edward had no clue at all what he wanted in life.

Finn picked up the phone. Edward had been calling him for days and now Finn was ready call to him.

He just wanted to know if there was a chance Edward would ever be open to knowing what he wanted in life. And even if there was a small chance that could happen then Finn wanted to help him, support him and make sure they were okay.

Edward didn't pick up.

Joanna and Eli grinned and looked at each other.

"What?" Finn asked.

Eli and Joanna both held his hands.

"You know that catalogue we gave you, what if I was to tell you there is someone very familiar who works there?" Joanna asked.

Finn shook his hands free and opened the last

page of the catalogue that detailed out all the names of the employees with their photos too. And he actually recognised one of the names, Claire worked at the antique place.

And it was open right now so Finn got up and he really wanted to talk to Claire. If anyone knew how to reach Edward it would hopefully be her.

But Finn knew that Albert was Claire's boyfriend so he just hoped Claire wasn't too upset about Saturday night and Edward breaking her boyfriend's nose.

If that happened then Finn knew he was screwed.

CHAPTER 18
28th March 2023
Oxford, England

Ever since Edward had seen how angry, upset and outraged Claire was at what had happened and what her dick of an ex-boyfriend had caused, Edward had felt so guilty about all of it. Him, Claire and Ivy couldn't sit in the common rooms anymore, they couldn't eat in the college dining halls and the entire situation was rubbish.

And all the guilt, fear and pain Edward had been feeling had all been leading to this single moment.

Edward sat in a very ancient and horrible-looking green leather chair from the 19th century as he sat in front of a large 20th century brown wooden desk. There was barely any natural light in the office because of the bad windows.

But in front of Edward was the College Dean, an elderly large man called Oliver Bramble and he just looked down at Edward like he was trash.

"Edward the scholarship kid. I have been waiting a while for this to happen but this is why I do not believe in scholarships at Oxford," Oliver said. "I believe that the privileged should come here and them alone,"

Edward shook his head. "Times have moved on, sir. Knowledge isn't only for the rich and powerful and I deserve any education like anyone else,"

"Normally I would agree with such a statement," Oliver said, "but you have proven a fundamental point about the middle and working class. You people are animals at heart, unintelligent creatures that respond to animal instincts too quickly. You got angry so you assaulted a first-class member of our society,"

Edward shook his head. "If you rich and snobbish people were so great then why was Albert the man in the wrong?"

"You really think right and wrong matters in the world," Oliver said smiling. "You really think morals matter in the world now. World hunger and war is wrong, if that concerns you go and start a charity but Oxford is a business first and foremost,"

Edward hated this idiot and any illusions he had been having about Oxford for the past three years just shattered. Oxford wasn't a kind, loving place that prized knowledge above all else.

Well maybe certain colleges were like that, no maybe a ton of them were. But Edward's college was old, traditional and they hated him.

"And it is the parents and students like Albert

that bring millions into Oxford and what do scholarships like you bring into us? I only give out scholarships as a tick box exercise so I can show that this college is equal and diverse and all that bullshit,"

Edward so badly wished he had been recording this but he wasn't smart enough. Maybe the Dean was right.

"Therefore Edward I am going to have to suspend you for two months for assaulting another student,"

Edward stood up. "But my final exams are in less than two months,"

Oliver shrugged. "Exactly. You will never graduate Oxford and I really hope that sends a message to all the other disrespectful middle-class students that they don't deserve Oxford,"

"And you Dean," Edward said leaning over the desk, "are a nasty, elitist monster that Oxford doesn't deserve, and I know your fellow Deans would be most pleased to know what our conversations have been,"

"Get out of my office," Oliver said, "and just enjoy your free time because you still have your dorm at least,"

Edward shook his head and just went out of the office and started walking down the long horrible corridor with its dark brown walls.

He took out his phone and was about to call Claire and Ivy because he seriously needed his scheming best friend at the moment, but he noticed that Finn had called him.

Edward stopped in his tracks. He couldn't believe that Finn wanted to hear from him, he hated him for not standing up for him, supporting their relationship and everything that Finn had done for him.

Finn had showed Edward that being gay, being in love and just being himself was the best thing ever and he wanted that feeling so badly again. He had to make things right and then he had to deal with the Dean, because he was getting his degree no matter what.

Edward dialled Ivy as he knew Claire would sadly be at work. She answered on the third ring and sounded out of breath.

"Hi," Ivy said sounding abnormally happy.

"What's up?" Edward asked. "You don't sound like yourself,"

Ivy laughed hard and sounded like she was about to make a sex noise or something and Edward realised she was with Ben and clearly having a much better time than he was.

"You're with Ben," Edward said really happy for her. It was about time she finally managed to get some dick.

Then Edward realised that was perfect because Ben had powerful parents and that could help him a lot more than he ever thought possible.

"Put him on," Edward said.

"Ed he isn't a bad guy. You don't need to yell at

him to protect me,"

"Ivy my beautiful scheming friend I need to talk to him now,"

Edward listened to Ivy mutter something under her breath and then she passed the phone over to Ben.

"Hello," he said.

Edward just grinned to himself as he was about to have the most important conversation in his life and he absolutely had to get Ben onboard no matter the cost.

His future depended on it.

CHAPTER 19
28th March 2023
Oxford, England

Finn really didn't like how the silly buses were late for a change around Oxford, it was only three minutes before closing as he entered the massive multi-storey antique shop in the centre of Oxford.

He couldn't believe his eyes as he saw endless rows upon rows of golden shiny objects, 1st edition books and so many antiques from so many time periods on shelves and in cabinets. Finn had never seen so many beautiful objects in all his life.

But all the objects were still nothing compared to beautiful, precious Edward. The man he wanted back so badly.

Joanna and Eli gently pushed him forward as Claire in a very tight-fitting black uniform came towards him.

"I didn't expect to see you here," Claire said weakly smiling. "How are you? And I cannot stress enough *how* sorry I am for what happened. He dumped me as soon as I started standing up for both of you,"

"At least you stood up for me," Finn said failing to hide the anger in his voice.

"Claire," a middle-aged man said, "we're closing. Tell the customers to come back tomorrow,"

Claire frowned at Finn. "Wait outside for ten minutes and I'll be there,"

Thirty minutes later, Finn bought them all diet cokes as they sat round a small round wooden table in a local pub he had never been in before. It was quiet for early evening but he liked it and it meant no one could overhear them.

"How's Edward?" Finn asked not knowing if he should ask or not but he couldn't help himself.

Claire took a long sip. "In a bad way really. He hates him, he hates that he hurt you, me and Ivy. He just hates himself,"

Finn hated how bad Edward felt, he never wanted his precious man to be in pain and this was a nightmare. He had to tell Edward that he didn't forgive him but he was willing to support him on the condition Edward agreed to tell him stuff.

Edward never should have kept his fear about the other Oxford students finding out a secret. Or he shouldn't have denied this relationship was real.

"How are you doing?" Joanna asked just a moment before Finn could.

Joanna folded her arms. "Me and Ivy were lost

and hurt about Saturday night. I was angry because I had been dating such a horrible snob, I was mad at Edward for not defending you and I was sad for you,"

Finn didn't understand. He had only just met Claire for ten seconds before the fight kicked off.

"Why?" he asked.

"Because me, Ivy and Edward have been friends for well over a decade. I've seen him at his best, his worst and I have met all his boyfriends. And the only boy he has ever treated as this special and careful is you. He loves you,"

Finn leant back into his chair. He couldn't believe it that Edward loved him and he still treated him like this.

"I need to see him," Finn said. "I know we can make things right,"

Claire nodded. "I don't disagree but Edward's not sure about anything because we all know how his meeting with the Dean's going to go. He will be suspended, sacked and then-"

Finn's phone buzzed. It was Edward. He answered it but then he realised it was a text.

"I'm no longer an Oxford student. I'm useless, pathetic and you deserve someone better. I'm sorry for everything I put you through but I'm no good to anyone," Finn said reading out the message.

Finn got up and hugged Claire as it was clear that she was as concerned as she was.

Then Finn got down on the sticky pub floor and

looked up at her, into her vibrant green eyes and grinned.

"Is there any way you can get me into Oxford?" Finn asked.

"Of course," Claire said laughing. "It isn't a prison. Non-students come in and out all the time. All you need is an ID card to get you into the place,"

"Please take me back with you. Let me talk to him because it's clear he's in a bad way," Finn said.

He wasn't sure if Claire was going to say anything for a moment but after a few moments she nodded and grinned.

"It would be my pleasure because I feel you're going to be the only person who can talk to him," Claire said, "and that means Ivy's going to be there too,"

They all got up and started walking out the pub as Finn asked, "Why does she need to be there?"

"Because my sister will want to see this so she can factor in this information to whatever schemes she has going on,"

"Your sister's weird," Finn said.

Finn loved it as Claire hugged him as they all left and then Joanna and Eli hugged him too.

And Finn realised that as long as he could convince Edward that everything would be okay that was going to be perfect. He had great friends, great support and now he just needed his great boyfriend to take him back.

But he knew that was going to be a lot harder

than he ever wanted to admit.

CHAPTER 20
28th March 2023
Oxford, England

As much as Edward loved how ancient Oxford was with its masonry buildings and dark wooden corridors that made him feel like he was walking into another time, he was glad the Oxford dorms were modern, bright and comfortable.

He just threw himself on the soft white bedsheets and he couldn't believe how bad his life was. He had tried and tried and tried to convince Ben to get him to call his parents in case they could help him, but he said he had wanted to help but his parents wouldn't help someone they didn't know.

Edward supposed it was sort of fair but he just hated the situation. He hated that his entire future was at risk all because some idiot had made fun of the man he loved, he knew violence and punching was wrong but Albert deserved it.

It was even worse that Claire and Ivy were

hurting and poor, sweet, sexy Finn. Edward really didn't want to know how the man he loved was doing because he knew the answer would be way too painful.

He had been a bad student, a horrible friend and a foul boyfriend. None of them deserved them so maybe he should just run away. Go somewhere else where no one knew him, where no one could be hurt by him and he could just start over.

It would be better for Claire, Ivy and Finn anyway. At least that way they could move on and meet a friend they actually deserved.

"Open up," Claire said pounding on the door.

Edward didn't move. Maybe she would just leave if he didn't make a sound for a few moments.

"I have someone who wants to see you," Claire said.

"I don't want to see anyone. You're all better off without me," Edward said. "I'm a terrible friend that just hurts everyone,"

"Maybe," Claire said. "I still love you and someone else here does too,"

"Let me in please," Finn said.

Edward shot up. His heart pounded in his chest. His hands turned sweaty.

Edward went over to the door and slowly opened it then Finn came inside with Claire and Ivy and Edward just didn't know what to move, think or do.

But he couldn't deny that Finn was so beautiful,

so perfect and so sexy. Edward focused on his slim body and that divine angelic face and Edward even dared himself to run his fingers through Finn's wonderfully pink hair.

He was so angelic, so divine and Finn was just the loveliest man on the planet.

"I don't know where to start," Edward said slowly wrapping his arms around the man he really, really loved. Edward loved Finn's sweet earthy aftershave expertly mixed with his own nervous sweat.

He was so cute.

"That makes two of us," Finn said, "but I want you to say sorry,"

Edward nodded. "I shouldn't have said or made you say anything at all. I was selfish and I was just thinking of myself and my position. Not that it matters at all,"

Edward saw Claire and Ivy gestured him to continue.

"I should have told you straight away what my fears were and I know they were silly. But I was so… nervous about this place. I think for three years I've been telling myself that this college was perfect and it was what I needed. But it wasn't,"

Edward loved it how Finn stroked his cheek gently.

"There are so many other better colleges that don't have Deans as dicks," Edward said moving closer to Finn and his wonderful lips. "And from now on I promise you are my first whatever. You are my boyfriend, you are my focus and you are my everything,"

Finn moved away and Edward let him.

"I mean it," Edward said. "When I watched you walk out the pub on Saturday it killed me. I hated hurting you and if you don't want to get back together I understand. I just want you to know how much I care about you,"

Finn looked him in the eye. "Do you have any idea how tough this was for me?"

"No," Edward said, "and I'm sorry I never thought about how this would affect you and yes, I was always scared of getting caught. But that's going to change now because I love you,"

Finn slowly came back over to him and Edward just hugged him. Edward didn't kiss him, feel his body or even run a finger through his hair. He wanted, needed Finn to know that he wasn't using him to get off or anything. All he wanted was for Finn to know how much he cared about him.

And he wouldn't blame Finn if he wanted to walk away or anything but he couldn't let Finn walk away from him unless he knew that first.

"I love you too," Finn said.

CHAPTER 21
29th March 2023
Oxford, England

Edward absolutely loved hugging, kissing and holding Finn's soft, wonderful hand in public as him and Finn had explored Oxford together as a real couple making sure everyone could see them.

And Edward had just flat out loved it.

In the evening, Edward and Finn and all their best friends finally met in Finn's living room for the first time. Edward was surprised at how amazing and great it looked with all its little design features and colours and textures.

Finn was seriously talented.

Edward hugged Finn tight and rested his head on top of Finn's as Joanna sat next to them and he realised him and Finn really should have bought some extra chairs today so they could finally have some good seating. But he supposed with everyone scrambling to sit on sofas, camping chairs and the floor, it just made the living room more homely.

It was even better that Ben had joined them as Ivy's official boyfriend, and that was the real point of tonight's social and dinner. They needed to make Ben's parents get involved in the university because it turned out they were actually on the Board of Directors and they were a lot richer than Albert's parents.

As Eli bought up in the large boxes of pizzas that made the entire house smelt delightful of bacon, sausage, mushrooms and so many other sensational smells, Edward smiled at Ben and everyone knew it was game time.

"So how do your parents find being on the Board of the uni?" Edward asked.

Ben shook his head. "I knew this was just a setup to make me intervene, but I am sorry Edward I don't really talk to my parents,"

"Why not?" Finn asked.

"Because my parents are very traditional, very rich and they have strong views about everything. Talking to them can quickly develop into an argument or something else entirely,"

Edward picked up a slice of sausage pizza that made Finn grin and he almost playfully hit his boyfriend on the head but he had to focus on Ben for now.

"Come on," Joanna said, "I know we don't go to Oxford but Edward is a great person, he's caring and a very dedicated student. And you know this suspension isn't right,"

Ben clicked his fingers. "Edward when's your Hearing date?"

Edward had no idea what he was talking about. All he knew was that he was suspended from the university for the next two months and that meant he had to miss his exams.

"I thought so," Ben said. "You might not need to go through my parents actually because I presume you would have gotten a real Suspension Letter through email or something,"

Edward nodded. He had hated hearing the very formal email and whatnot.

"Well," Ben said, "if you print off the email and take it to the Head of the University then she'll show you that the Suspension isn't real. Because she didn't sign it and she cannot sign off on a suspension until she's heard both sides of the argument,"

Edward felt really numb as he realised what was going on. He was on a fake suspension that didn't mean anything and that meant he could still get his degree, do and pass his exams and then he could do whatever he wanted with his life.

He could live the life he had always wanted with sexy Finn by his side.

Edward hugged Finn so tight. Finn coughed but Edward didn't care.

Everything was finally right with the world. He had fixed the mistake with his friends so Claire was no longer in a bad relationship, he had made a bunch of new friends in the form of Joanna and Eli and most importantly, he had met the love of his life.

And that was something Edward had really noticed over the past few weeks. Whenever he was with sexy, precious, angelic Finn Edward felt alive and light and like he could actually take on the world.

That was a precious feeling to have and now that everything was okay, because tomorrow morning he was going to print off that email and expose the Dean for the idiot he was, Edward was really looking forward to sharing the rest of his life with his friends and beautiful Finn.

The beautiful man he never expected to fall in love with but he was so glad that he had.

CHAPTER 22
23rd June 2023
Oxford, London

Over the past three months, Finn had absolutely loved every single second of his time with Edward. They basically spent every night together and as soon as the head of Oxford University had discovered what the Dean had done, Oliver had been fired and blacklisted from the world of academia.

Finn was really pleased that the university had wanted to pay Edward compensation in exchange for his silence on the matter, and he was so glad that his boyfriend had accepted it.

And after watching Edward graduate from Oxford with a First-Class degree, Finn was so glad, lucky and proud of his boyfriend. He was the luckiest man in the world to end up with a man like Edward who was smart, caring and amazing in bed. Finn was so looking forward to having sex again later as they continued celebrating Edward's graduation.

Finn sat on a very comfortable and slightly modern black sofa in the now-completed living room with Edward resting his head on his lap. The silence between them wasn't awkward or weird or anything even remotely negative, it was the sort of gentle silence between lovers that knew they didn't always need to be talking to be intimate.

Finn really liked how the bright baby blue walls of the living room really did add some light, airy textures to the space that was immediately contrasted with the ancient, dark bookshelves with dents, cuts and knocks in them. They were well-aged and beautiful and he was even more pleased with all the fake golden and "rusted" and bronzed relics that he had placed in-between the books and on shelves.

It had been amazing to watch Joanna and Eli run away inspecting everything like children when he had first unveiled it to them. Finn loved seeing his best friends so happy and it was even better that both of them were out on a date with each other together.

Finn supposed it had made perfect sense because they had gone shopping together, spend tons of time together and they were just great together. Finn couldn't have been happier for them and he really knew that their own relationship would be beyond perfect.

Just like his and Edward's.

As Finn enjoyed the silence between them and enjoyed the faint scent of Edward's expensive spicy aftershave that made Edward's taste form on his tongue. Finn gently stroked his boyfriend's hair and he never wanted to be apart from Edward.

Something that wouldn't be happening anymore because Edward was going to do a Masters at Oxford and Finn was really glad about that. It meant they could live together in this house, *their* house in reality, and they could always be together. Exactly how they were meant to be.

"I am glad you came here to Oxford," Edward said getting up and cuddling up close to Finn. "I can't imagine my life without you,"

Finn kissed Edward slowly and tenderly. "I don't want to imagine my life without you either. But what do you think our bedroom should look like?"

Edward laughed beautifully and Finn kissed him a few more times until he was somehow on top of Edward.

"You just finished your living room and you're starting a new design job next month,"

Finn grinned. He was so damn glad he had finally found an interior design firm in Oxford that had liked his dedication to making sure the space reflected the client, how he cut corners to create an amazing space for a cheaper price and how they respected his own sense of style in his own home.

He knew life really was perfect at this point. He had great friends, a great new job that was going to be exactly what he had always wanted, and he finally had a boyfriend that would always love him, treasure him and support him.

Exactly what he would do to him.

As Edward rolled his eyes towards the door so they could go upstairs for adult celebrations, Finn grabbed his hands and kissed him tenderly, slowly and lovingly because he was so damn lucky.

As a child he might have wanted to come to Oxford for the sights, to work and to party because it was the city of dreaming spires, but Finn never ever expected to fall for Oxford itself.

It was a beautiful city with the most beautiful men imaginable.

GET YOUR FREE SHORT STORY NOW!

And get signed up to Connor Whiteley's newsletter to hear about new gripping books, offers and exciting projects. (You'll never be sent spam)

https://www.subscribepage.com/gayromancesignup

About the author:

Connor Whiteley is the author of over 60 books in the sci-fi fantasy, nonfiction psychology and books for writer's genre and he is a Human Branding Speaker and Consultant.

He is a passionate warhammer 40,000 reader, psychology student and author.

Who narrates his own audiobooks and he hosts The Psychology World Podcast.

All whilst studying Psychology at the University of Kent, England.

Also, he was a former Explorer Scout where he gave a speech to the Maltese President in August 2018 and he attended Prince Charles' 70th Birthday Party at Buckingham Palace in May 2018.

Plus, he is a self-confessed coffee lover!

Other books by Connor Whiteley:
Bettie English Private Eye Series
A Very Private Woman
The Russian Case
A Very Urgent Matter
A Case Most Personal
Trains, Scots and Private Eyes
The Federation Protects
Cops, Robbers and Private Eyes
Just Ask Bettie English
An Inheritance To Die For
The Death of Graham Adams
Bearing Witness
The Twelve
The Wrong Body
The Assassination Of Bettie English
Wining And Dying
Eight Hours
Uniformed Cabal
A Case Most Christmas

Gay Romance Novellas
Breaking, Nursing, Repairing A Broken Heart
Jacob And Daniel
Fallen For A Lie
Spying And Weddings
Clean Break

Awakening Love
Meeting A Country Man
Loving Prime Minister
Snowed In Love
Never Been Kissed
Love Betrays You

<u>Lord of War Origin Trilogy:</u>
Not Scared Of The Dark
Madness
Burn Them All

<u>The Fireheart Fantasy Series</u>
Heart of Fire
Heart of Lies
Heart of Prophecy
Heart of Bones
Heart of Fate

<u>City of Assassins (Urban Fantasy)</u>
City of Death
City of Marytrs
City of Pleasure
City of Power

Agents of The Emperor
Return of The Ancient Ones
Vigilance
Angels of Fire
Kingmaker
The Eight
The Lost Generation
Hunt
Emperor's Council
Speaker of Treachery
Birth Of The Empire
Terraforma
Spaceguard

The Rising Augusta Fantasy Adventure Series
Rise To Power
Rising Walls
Rising Force
Rising Realm

Lord Of War Trilogy (Agents of The Emperor)
Not Scared Of The Dark
Madness
Burn It All Down

Miscellaneous:
RETURN
FREEDOM
SALVATION
Reflection of Mount Flame
The Masked One
The Great Deer
English Independence

OTHER SHORT STORIES BY CONNOR WHITELEY

Mystery Short Story Collections
Criminally Good Stories Volume 1: 20 Detective Mystery Short Stories
Criminally Good Stories Volume 2: 20 Private Investigator Short Stories
Criminally Good Stories Volume 3: 20 Crime Fiction Short Stories
Criminally Good Stories Volume 4: 20 Science Fiction and Fantasy Mystery Short Stories
Criminally Good Stories Volume 5: 20 Romantic Suspense Short Stories

Mystery Short Stories:
Protecting The Woman She Hated
Finding A Royal Friend

Our Woman In Paris
Corrupt Driving
A Prime Assassination
Jubilee Thief
Jubilee, Terror, Celebrations
Negative Jubilation
Ghostly Jubilation
Killing For Womenkind
A Snowy Death
Miracle Of Death
A Spy In Rome
The 12:30 To St Pancreas
A Country In Trouble
A Smokey Way To Go
A Spicy Way To GO
A Marketing Way To Go
A Missing Way To Go
A Showering Way To Go
Poison In The Candy Cane
Kendra Detective Mystery Collection Volume 1
Kendra Detective Mystery Collection Volume 2
Mystery Short Story Collection Volume 1
Mystery Short Story Collection Volume 2
Criminal Performance
Candy Detectives

Key To Birth In The Past

<u>Fantasy Short Stories:</u>
City of Snow
City of Light
City of Vengeance
Dragons, Goats and Kingdom
Smog The Pathetic Dragon
Don't Go In The Shed
The Tomato Saver
The Remarkable Way She Died
Dragon Coins
Dragon Tea
Dragon Rider

<u>All books in 'An Introductory Series':</u>
Careers In Psychology
Psychology of Suicide
Dementia Psychology
Clinical Psychology Reflections Volume 4
Forensic Psychology of Terrorism And Hostage-Taking
Forensic Psychology of False Allegations
Year In Psychology
CBT For Anxiety
CBT For Depression
Applied Psychology

BIOLOGICAL PSYCHOLOGY 3RD EDITION
COGNITIVE PSYCHOLOGY THIRD EDITION
SOCIAL PSYCHOLOGY- 3RD EDITION
ABNORMAL PSYCHOLOGY 3RD EDITION
PSYCHOLOGY OF RELATIONSHIPS- 3RD EDITION
DEVELOPMENTAL PSYCHOLOGY 3RD EDITION
HEALTH PSYCHOLOGY
RESEARCH IN PSYCHOLOGY
A GUIDE TO MENTAL HEALTH AND TREATMENT AROUND THE WORLD- A GLOBAL LOOK AT DEPRESSION
FORENSIC PSYCHOLOGY
THE FORENSIC PSYCHOLOGY OF THEFT, BURGLARY AND OTHER CRIMES AGAINST PROPERTY
CRIMINAL PROFILING: A FORENSIC PSYCHOLOGY GUIDE TO FBI PROFILING AND GEOGRAPHICAL AND STATISTICAL PROFILING.
CLINICAL PSYCHOLOGY
FORMULATION IN PSYCHOTHERAPY
PERSONALITY PSYCHOLOGY AND

INDIVIDUAL DIFFERENCES
CLINICAL PSYCHOLOGY REFLECTIONS VOLUME 1
CLINICAL PSYCHOLOGY REFLECTIONS VOLUME 2
Clinical Psychology Reflections Volume 3
CULT PSYCHOLOGY
Police Psychology

A Psychology Student's Guide To University
How Does University Work?
A Student's Guide To University And Learning
University Mental Health and Mindset

www.ingramcontent.com/pod-product-compliance
Lightning Source LLC
LaVergne TN
LVHW012112070526
838202LV00056B/5700